# Aberdeenshire
## COUNCIL

To Myla, from the fairies

Special thanks to
Rachel Elliot

ORCHARD BOOKS
338 Euston Road, London NW1 3BH
Orchard Books Australia
Level 17/207 Kent Street, Sydney, NSW 2000
A Paperback Original

First published in 2013 by Orchard Books

A CIP catalogue record for this book is available
from the British Library.

ISBN 978 1 40832 796 8

1 3 5 7 9 10 8 6 4 2

Printed in Great Britain

The paper and board used in this paperback are natural recyclable
products made from wood grown in sustainable forests. The
manufacturing processes conform to the environmental regulations
of the country of origin.

Orchard Books is a division of Hachette Children's Books,
an Hachette UK company

www.hachette.co.uk

# Savannah
## the Zebra
## Fairy

by Daisy Meadows

ORCHARD

www.rainbowmagic.co.uk

The Fairyland
Palace

Meadow

Stream

Beehive

Arctic Tundra

Eucalyptus
Forest

Tropical Waterfall

Wild Woods
Nature
Reserve

Jack Frost's
Ice Castle

To Jack Frost's Zoo

Watering Hole

Pagoda

Desert Oasis

Jack Frost's Spell

I love animals, yes I do,
I want my very own private zoo!
I'll capture the animals one by one,
With fairy magic to help me on!

A koala, a tiger, an Arctic fox,
I'll keep them in cages with giant locks.
Every kind of animal will be there,
A panda, a meerkat, a honey bear.
The animals will be my property,
I'll be master of a huge menagerie!

# Contents

# A Deer Display

"I wonder what junior ranger badges we'll earn today," said Rachel Walker as she got out of the car at the Wild Woods Nature Reserve.

"I hope we'll be spending time with the animals again," said her best friend Kirsty Tate. "Since the fairies gave us the gift of being able to understand what animals say, I want to be with them the whole time!"

The girls smiled at each other happily. As friends of Fairyland, they were used to magical adventures. But this summer they were having a non-magical adventure too. They were spending a week as volunteer junior rangers at Wild Woods Nature Reserve. Every day, the junior rangers earned badges for their backpacks by doing jobs around the reserve. Rachel and Kirsty had already earned three badges for their backpacks.

"This week is going so fast," said Rachel. "I can't believe it's already our fourth day!"

"Look, there's Becky," said Kirsty, seeing the manager of the reserve walking towards them. "Come on, let's find out what she wants us to do today."

The girls waved goodbye to Mrs Tate,

who had driven them to the nature reserve.

"Good morning, girls!" said Becky. "I've got a lovely job for you this morning. I want you to feed our herd of deer. They're some of the sweetest animals on the reserve, and there's a baby fawn  that's especially cute, although he's very shy so you might not see him."

The girls could hardly believe their ears. The beautiful deer were one of the main visitor attractions at the reserve.

"Really?" Rachel gasped. "Thank you, Becky!"

"It's like a dream come true!" said Kirsty.

"Well, let's get started then!" said Becky with a laugh.

She led the girls over to where four large buckets were waiting on the ground.

"These are full of deer feed," said Becky.

"What do the deer eat?" asked Kirsty, peering into the buckets.

"It's a special mixture of fruit and grasses," Becky told them.

"The visitors love to watch them being fed every day."

"Why do the deer have to be fed by humans?" Rachel asked. "Isn't there enough food for them growing at the nature reserve?"

"That's a really good question," said Becky. "There's plenty of food for the deer growing here, but we do a special daily feeding display for the visitors so that they can see the animals close up."

Carrying two buckets each, the girls followed Becky to a pretty meadow, full of clover and buttercups. On the far side of the meadow was a leafy wood, and a fence surrounded the other three sides. There were lots of people standing beside the fence. They looked excited and hopeful.

"Look, the visitors are gathering already," said Becky. "I'll go over and talk to them while you scatter the food around. The deer will be here soon – they know when it's feeding time!"

She walked over to the fence, and Rachel and Kirsty made their way slowly through the meadow towards the wood, scattering the deer feed as they went.

"My heart's thumping like mad," said Kirsty in a whisper. "We're actually going to see real-life deer!"

"Look!" said Rachel in a thrilled voice.

Two deer were stepping out of the wood and into the meadow. One was a velvet-soft female, and the other was a buck with large antlers. They moved with great grace, and their big eyes blinked shyly as they looked at the girls.

Kirsty smiled and scattered a little more food. The animals moved closer. Then more of the herd came out from between the trees. Soon the girls were surrounded by lots of deer wanting food.

"Listen," said Kirsty. "They're whispering to each other!"

"Not many visitors today," the girls heard one buck saying to another.

"Tuck in, everybody," said a third.

"Mmm, scrumptious clover," murmured a young female deer behind Rachel.

"I'm so glad that you like it," said Rachel in a soft voice.

The deer all pricked up their ears and stared at her with interest.

"How unusual," said an older female. "Humans who really know how to communicate!"

"We're friends with the fairies," Kirsty explained to them. "They gave us the magical power of being able to talk to animals."

17

"It was the best gift ever," Rachel added.

"Yes," said Kirsty thoughtfully, turning to her best friend. "But we mustn't forget *why* they gave it to us. We promised to help protect the animals from Jack Frost and his goblins! We can't let him take animals from the wild – they're not just objects to be collected."

On their first day at Wild Woods Nature Reserve, the girls had travelled to Fairyland and met the Baby Animal Rescue Fairies, who looked after animals in both Fairyland and in the human world. While they were there, Jack Frost had stolen the fairies' magical key rings and ordered his goblins to bring him lots of animals from the human world. He wanted to put them in a private zoo for his own selfish enjoyment. Kirsty and Rachel had vowed to stop him and the fairies had given them the power to talk to animals.

"We've already saved a panda, a tiger and a meerkat," said Rachel. "I wonder if the fairies will need our help again today!"

# Fairy in Hiding!

The girls scattered some more feed around the meadow.

"I hope you enjoy your meal," said Kirsty, smiling at the deer.

"It's nice to meet some humans who really understand us," said a handsome buck. "The others who work here are very nice, but they don't always seem to know what we want."

"Do you like living at the reserve?" asked Rachel.

"It's wonderful here," said the buck. "All the food we can eat, and huge, tree-filled areas to live in. It's perfect."

The girls smiled, and Kirsty took off her blue-and-white sun hat and wiped her forehead. The day was getting hotter and hotter. The hat slipped out of her hand and fell onto the

ground. Before Kirsty could pick it up, the handsome buck had trodden on it by accident.

"I'm very sorry," he said, lifting his hoof.

"I hope I haven't spoiled it."

"Oh no, it's fine," said Kirsty. She picked it up and hooked it over a twig on a tree at the edge of the wood for safekeeping.

Rachel was gazing around at the deer who were happily feeding. A different buck gently nudged her with his antlers. "There appears to be a little more food in that bucket..." he remarked.

Rachel laughed and bent down to empty the rest of the food onto the grass. As she straightened up, she saw a movement among the trees in front of her.

"Kirsty, look over there," she whispered. "I think it's the baby fawn that Becky was talking about."

Both girls peered over to where a small, dappled fawn was trying to hide behind a tree.

"Oh, he's shy," said Kirsty.

She held out her hand and walked towards the fawn.

"Leave some for the others, okay?"
Rachel said to the buck, with a grin.

She followed Kirsty towards the trees.

"There's some lovely food over here,"
Kirsty was saying in a soft voice. "Why
don't you come and try some?"

The little fawn took a few steps back.

"There's plenty to
go around," said
Rachel.

But the
fawn hid his
face behind
a large
bush.

"Don't be
scared," said
Kirsty in a kind
voice.

25

At that moment, Rachel heard a faint, tinkling voice. She put her hand on Kirsty's arm.

"Listen!" she said.

"Rachel!" came the voice again. "Kirsty!"

"It's a fairy!" said Kirsty.

The girls looked around, trying to follow the sound of the voice.

"It's coming from your sun hat!" said Rachel.

They ran over to the tree where Kirsty had hung her hat, but there was no one there.

"I'm sure that it came from over here," said Rachel, feeling confused.

They heard a tiny, bell-like giggle.

"It's nice to see you again," said the voice.

Kirsty peered more closely at her hat, and then a big smile spread across her face.

"It's Savannah the Zebra Fairy!" she said.

It was no wonder that Savannah could hardly be seen against the blue-and-white stripes of the hat. She was wearing a blue-striped tunic dress with dark leggings. Her reddish-brown hair glinted in the sunlight as she hovered just in front them.

27

"Hello, Savannah!" said Rachel in an excited voice. "We almost didn't see you."

"My stripes camouflage me," said Savannah, turning a little pirouette against the backdrop of the hat. "See! None of the human visitors can see me, even though I'm in full view."

"That's amazing," said Kirsty, looking at all the visitors. "Some of them are looking right at you, Savannah. That's so clever."

"I learned it from my friends the zebras," said Savannah. "They have stripes that camouflage them in the jungle."

"It would be amazing to see a real zebra," said Rachel.

"Actually, I've come to ask if you'd

like to come and see some right now," said Savannah. "You see, there are some goblins chasing them and they're getting scared... I would really appreciate your help."

"We'll come straight away!" said Kirsty.

# Stampede!

"We'll do anything we can to stop Jack Frost and his goblins," said Rachel.

The girls glanced back at the deer. They were finishing the food the girls had scattered. Becky was still talking to the visitors, and no one was looking at the girls. They slipped behind the tree where the fawn had hidden.

Savannah lifted her wand and waved it over the girls in a zigzag pattern. Instantly, they felt the power of Savannah's magic sweep them into the air, and the trees around them disappeared.

"I feel as if I've walked into a sauna," said Kirsty, looking around. "Wow, where are we?"

They were standing on a grassy plain, which stretched so far in all directions that the girls couldn't see where it began or ended. The sky was bright blue, and everything shimmered in the heat.

"What's that noise?" asked Rachel.

Savannah and Kirsty listened. They could hear a thundering roar, which seemed to be getting louder. Then Kirsty turned around, and gave a yell.

"Stampede!"

A herd of zebras was pounding towards them across the plain!

Savannah waved her wand again and the girls were transformed into fairies. In the blink of an eye they were zooming upwards, their wings fluttering so fast that they were blurs.

They were only just in time! They
felt a rush of air as the herd of zebras
charged underneath them.

"Look!" cried Rachel, pointing to the
back of the stampede.

A baby zebra was scampering along,
trying to keep up.

"He looks scared," said Savannah. "Come on, let's go and see him."

She led Rachel and Kirsty over the crowd of zebras until they were flying alongside the baby zebra.

"Hello, little one," said Savannah. "These are my friends Rachel and Kirsty. Why are you all running?"

"I'm Ziggy," said the little zebra in a breathless voice.

"Haven't you seen the strange green things? They're scary!"

Two adult zebras slowed down and trotted back to Ziggy.

"Mum, Dad!" cried Ziggy. "I'm glad to see you! Look, I made some new friends!"

"Ziggy, you have to stay with the herd," said his mother. "It's dangerous to be alone when those strange creatures are around."

"What were they like?" asked Savannah.

"There were four of them," said Ziggy's father. "Green creatures with enormous feet and long noses."

Rachel and Kirsty exchanged a suspicious glance.

"That sounds like goblins," said Rachel.

"Maybe if we follow the zebras' hoofprints back the way they came, we might find the goblins," said Kirsty.

"Great plan!" Savannah said, turning around with a determined expression.

The three friends rose high above the grassy plain, following the zebras' hoofprints backwards. They flew a long way, tracking the prints back across the grass. They flew over wide-spreading trees and then Rachel gave a yell.

"Look – down there!" she cried.

Two goblins were sitting beside a watering hole, holding a big brown sack.

The girls fluttered down and hid in the long grass around the watering hole. The goblins were talking loudly, not thinking that anyone could be listening. They made a funny-looking pair, because one of them was very tall and skinny, like a beanpole, and the other was short and podgy, like a pudding.

"We have to catch the baby zebra before those other two idiots," said the podgy goblin.

"Who is he talking about?" asked Rachel in a whisper. "Who else could be trying to catch Ziggy?"

"Ziggy's parents said that they had seen four green creatures," Kirsty remembered. "There must be two more goblins around here somewhere. Perhaps they're having a competition to see who can catch Ziggy first."

"Those mean goblins!" said Savannah.

"The others have got that fairy's key ring toy to help them catch the zebra," said the skinny goblin in a gloomy voice. "We don't stand a chance."

"Don't talk rubbish," said the podgy goblin. "We've got a bag full of zebra traps, and all they've got is that stupid fluffy toy."

He opened the sack and pulled out a

large net, herbs and twigs to attract the zebra and a rope tied at the end like a lasso.

"Jack Frost will be very pleased with us when we bring him that baby zebra," the podgy goblin went on. "He'll probably give us a big reward."

Kirsty put her hand over her mouth, looking upset.

"They're planning to use those horrible things to catch Ziggy!" she said in a low voice. "We've got to stop them!"

# A Zany Zebra

Rachel was thinking about Ziggy running along with his family. Suddenly she had an idea.

"Savannah, can you magic up the sound of a zebra stampede?" she asked. "If we can make the goblins think that they can hear the zebras, maybe we can send them away from where Ziggy really is."

"That's a great idea," said Savannah.

She waved her wand, and suddenly the girls heard the thunder of zebra hooves. The sound was coming from the opposite direction to where the zebras really were.

"Listen!" said the skinny goblin, sitting up very straight. "That's the zebras – it's coming from over there! Come on!"

They stuffed their equipment back into the sack and ran off with it – far away from the zebras!

Rachel, Kirsty and Savannah burst into laughter.

"That's two goblins out of the way," said Kirsty.

"Which leaves two more to find, as well as Savannah's key ring," said Rachel.

"Let's go back and check on Ziggy,"

Savannah suggested.

The three friends zoomed upwards, enjoying the warmth of the sun on their wings. They flew back across the grassy plain to the zebras. The herd had stopped running, and they were grazing on the juicy grass.

Kirsty and Rachel spiralled downwards, followed by Savannah.

"All I can see is black and white," said Rachel with a laugh.

45

"And green," said Kirsty in a worried voice. "Look at that zebra over there. It's got *green*-and-white stripes!"

The strange-looking zebra was in the centre of the herd, moving steadily towards Ziggy and his parents.

Savannah frowned and waved her wand. All their outfits changed, and they were now each wearing a black-and-white tunic dress.

"The stripes will help to camouflage us," the little fairy explained. "Come on – we have to save Ziggy!"

They swooped down and landed on Ziggy's back. But he didn't seem to notice them. He was moving through the crowd of zebras, faster and faster, leaving his parents behind. Rachel stood up on his back and peered ahead.

"He's moving towards the green-and-white zebra," she said.

Kirsty stood up too, and she and Rachel held hands.

Ziggy was galloping now, and they had to flutter their wings to keep their balance.

"Look at the green zebra's feet," said Savannah. "They're enormous!"

They were very close now. Suddenly they heard a grumbling voice coming from the back end of the zebra.

"What's going on?" said the voice. "Haven't you got that zebra yet?"

"That's not a zebra," said Rachel. "It's two goblins in disguise!"

There was a muffled squawk from the front end of the zebra.

"The goblin at the front must have something in his mouth," said Rachel.

"I bet it's Savannah's magical key ring," said Kirsty in excitement. "That must be why Ziggy's following it.

They're using the toy to get Ziggy away from the herd."

"How are we going to get it back from inside a zebra costume?" asked Savannah.

She sounded defeated. Rachel and Kirsty squeezed her hands.

"I've got an idea," said Kirsty. "If all the zebras go for a drink at the watering hole, the goblin zebra will have to open its mouth to drink…"

"And it'll drop the toy," finished Rachel. "Brilliant idea, Kirsty!"

"But how can we get the zebras to go for a drink?" Kirsty asked. "Can you cast a spell, Savannah?"

Savannah laughed.

"There's no need for magic," she said. "The zebras are our friends. All we have to do is ask."

The girls split up and flitted among the zebras, asking each one to head for the watering hole. They flew low and stayed close to the zebras so that the goblins didn't spot them. A few minutes later, the whole herd set off for the watering hole. At first they trotted and then they started to run, their hooves pounding and shaking the ground. They ran faster and faster, and soon only two zebras were lagging behind – the goblin zebra...and Ziggy.

# Roped In!

By the time the goblins reached the
watering hole, most of the other zebras
had already finished drinking. The front
goblin trotted up to the hole and dipped
its head. Savannah's magical key ring
dropped into the shallow water.

"There it is!" said Kirsty. "Come on!"

The three girls swooped off Ziggy's back and darted down to the water, but then a hand reached out from the middle of the zebra costume. It was the goblin who was disguised as the back legs of the zebra, and he snatched the toy from under their hands.

"Fairies!" he yelled. "Pesky fairies! RUN!"

The front goblin panicked and ran in one direction, while the back goblin darted another way.

"This way, you stupid idiot!" squealed the front goblin.

54

The pretend zebra stumbled off across the grassland, followed by Ziggy.

"Ziggy, come back!" cried Rachel.

The fairies flew after them at top speed.

"Even if we catch those rotten goblins, how can we stop them?" asked Kirsty.

"I wish we had the lasso those other goblins had!" puffed Rachel.

Savannah grinned and waved her wand. Instantly, a long lasso appeared in Rachel's hands.

"Brilliant!" said Rachel.

With Kirsty and Savannah holding the other end of the rope, she whirled the lasso in the air and then aimed it at the goblin zebra. Could she make the throw?

Rachel flung the lasso over the pretend zebra's front end and pulled it tight. Then she flew around and coiled the

rope around its back legs. The goblins
were caught! Frightened, Ziggy gave a
cry of alarm and ran back to his parents
and the herd. The goblins struggled
in the lasso, and the pretend zebra
head came off and flopped to one side.
Underneath was a very hot, very cross-
looking goblin. He wriggled, but his arms
were trapped at his sides by the lasso.

"Let us go!" he squawked. "You'll be
sorry if you don't!"

"We're not scared of your threats," Kirsty replied.

The back end of the green-and-white zebra wiggled from side to side.

"I can't move!" came a muffled wail from the zebra's bottom. "Set my legs free!"

"Give us back Savannah's key ring first," said Rachel. "Then we'll let you go."

The goblins blew two enormous raspberries in reply.

"All right," said Rachel. "We can't force you to give the key ring back. But we can't let you hurt Ziggy either. So we'll just have to tie you up until we can be sure that Ziggy is safe."

She winked at Kirsty and Savannah, and started to wind the rope around the goblins some more.

"Stop that!" shrieked the front goblin.

"I can't move!" wailed the back goblin. "Let us go!"

"Give Savannah her magical key ring and then you can go free," said Rachel.

"Jack Frost will be so cross if we go back without the zebra," wailed the back goblin.

"He'll be even crosser if we don't go back at all," said the front goblin.

59

"Besides, it's teatime and I'm hungry. Give the silly fairy what she wants and let's get out of here."

Making loud grumbling noises, the back goblin put one hand out of the bottom of the costume and threw the magical key ring at Savannah. She caught it, and at once it returned to fairy-size.

Rachel let go of the rope and the goblins shook themselves free. The front goblin scowled at the fairies and put the pretend zebra head back on.

60

"Let's get back to the Ice Castle," he said. "I'm sick of zebras and I'm sick of fairies."

The goblins staggered away, still in their green-and-white costume.

"Let's go and check that Ziggy's okay," said Savannah.

The three fairies zipped back to the watering hole, where all the zebras were waiting for them. Savannah fluttered over to Ziggy, who was breathing heavily. She stroked his velvety muzzle and whispered to him. Steadily, his breathing slowed down and he started to look happier.

Ziggy's mother trotted over to where Rachel and Kirsty were hovering in the air.

"Thank you so much for helping to protect my son," she said. "We will never forget what you did for us today."

The whole herd gave the fairies three cheers, and then Savannah put her arms around Rachel and Kirsty.

"It's time for you to go back to the nature reserve," she said. "There are animals there who need you too."

# A Magic Touch

Savannah waved her wand, and in the blink of an eye the girls found themselves behind the tree in the meadow at Wild Woods Nature Reserve. Rachel and Kirsty looked around. The deer were still eating, the visitors were still listening to Becky's talk and the cute little fawn was still too shy to come out from behind the trees. Kirsty reached up and took her hat down from the tree.

"No time has passed since you left," said Savannah. "No one noticed anything. Girls, I can't thank you enough for helping me to find my magical key ring. And it will really cheer up the other Baby Animal Rescue Fairies to hear what happened today."

"Are you going back to Fairyland now?" Kirsty asked.

Savannah nodded. "I'm so happy that the zebras are safe," she said. "I hope you enjoy the rest of the week here, girls."

Savannah gave the girls a tiny butterfly kiss and then raised her wand. She made a zigzag in the air, and black-and-white fairydust fell all around her. When the sparkles cleared, she had disappeared.

"I'm so glad that we were able to help Savannah," said Rachel. "I just wish that we could help that shy little fawn too."

"Perhaps we can," said Kirsty. "Remember how Savannah calmed Ziggy down?"

She turned to the fawn, who trembled as she stepped closer to him.

67

"Hello," she said. "My name's Kirsty."
She reached out her hand and very,
very gently stroked his nose. The fawn
shifted his feet around, but he seemed to
like the attention.

"Don't be afraid," Kirsty said in a soft
voice. "We're your friends. All those
people waiting to see you are your
friends too."

The fawn tilted his head to one side, then nibbled at her sun hat. Kirsty giggled and pulled it away from him. Rachel fetched a handful of feed and held it out to him.

"Come on," she said in a gentle voice. "Come into the open."

Slowly, Rachel and Kirsty led the little fawn out into the meadow. Step by step he got nearer to the fence, nibbling tasty treats from Rachel's hand as he walked.

The visitors had noticed what the girls were doing, and were watching in breathless silence. The little fawn looked over at all the curious faces staring at him. He looked at Rachel and Kirsty, and they gave him reassuring smiles and nods. The fawn's head went up, and then he trotted over to the fence to say hello to the visitors.

"You two have a magic touch with animals," said Becky, walking over to them. "No one else has been able to get that little fawn into the open."

Rachel and Kirsty shared a secret smile. Becky had no idea that she was speaking the absolute truth!

"Thank you for doing such a wonderful job this morning," Becky went on. "Here are your badges."

She handed each of them a badge with a picture of a deer on to put on their backpacks.

"Thank you!" said the girls together.

As they walked across the meadow to collect the empty feed buckets, Rachel squeezed her best friend's hand.

"I wonder what kind of animal we'll be helping next," she said.

"Whatever it is, it'll be amazing," Kirsty replied. "I can't wait!"

Now it's time for Kirsty and
Rachel to help...

# Kimberley the Koala Fairy

**Read on for a sneak peek...**

"So here we are again at Wild Woods.
Maybe we'll get another badge today,"
Kirsty Tate said hopefully, smiling at her
best friend, Rachel Walker.

The girls were outside the wildlife
centre with the other junior rangers,
waiting for Becky, the head of the
Wild Woods Nature Reserve. Rachel
and Kirsty had volunteered to spend a
week of their summer holidays working
at the reserve, which was near Kirsty's
home, and every day Becky gave the
junior rangers a job to do. If the tasks

were successfully completed, they each received a badge.

"It would be *brilliant* to get another one!" Rachel exclaimed, patting her backpack proudly. The girls' hard work had already earned them four badges, and they'd pinned them to the pockets of their backpacks. "It's great to know that we're helping wildlife, and it's really fun, too."

"And helping out at Wild Woods isn't our *only* job this week," Kirsty reminded Rachel. "We're helping the Baby Animal Rescue Fairies, too!"

Read **Kimberley the Koala Fairy** to find out what adventures are in store for Kirsty and Rachel!

# Meet the
# Baby Animal Rescue Fairies

The Baby Animal Rescue Fairies have lost all their magical items. But luckily, Kirsty and Rachel are there to save the day and make sure all baby animals in the world are safe and sound.

## www.rainbowmagicbooks.co.uk

Look out for the next sparkly
Rainbow Magic Special!

# Robyn the Christmas Party Fairy

Rachel and Kirsty are helping to organise a big Christmas party.
But Jack Frost has stolen Robyn the Christmas Party Fairy's
magical objects! The girls must help Robyn,
before the spirit of Christmas is lost forever...

## Out now!

RAINBOW magic

Meet the fairies, play games
and get sneak peeks at
the latest books!

## www.rainbowmagicbooks.co.uk

There's fairy fun for everyone on
our wonderful website.
You'll find great activities, competitions, stories and
fairy profiles, and also a special newsletter.

Get 30% off all Rainbow Magic books at
## www.rainbowmagicbooks.co.uk

Enter the code RAINBOW at the checkout.
Offer ends 31 December 2013.

Offer valid in United Kingdom and Republic of Ireland only.

# Competition!

The Baby Animal Rescue Fairies have created
a special competition just for you!
In the back of each book in the series there will be
a question for you to answer.
Once you have collected all the books and all
seven answers, go online and enter the competition!

We will put all the correct entries into a draw and select
a winner to receive a special Rainbow Magic Goody Bag,
featuring lots of treats for you and your fairy friends.
The winner will also star in a new Rainbow Magic story!

**Which Fairy in the Pet Keeper
series has a pet kitten?**

_ _ _ _ _

## Enter online now at www.rainbowmagicbooks.co.uk

# Meet the
# Rainbow Fairies

Also available
as an ebook

Collect the seven original Rainbow Fairies
to find out how the adventure began!

# www.rainbowmagicbooks.co.uk

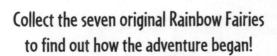